WHILE HALF THE WORLD IS SLEEPING

GABRIEL ANTHONY LOPEZ

Inquiries and Book Orders should be addressed to:

Great Writers Media
Email: info@greatwritersmedia.com
Phone: 877-600-5469

ISBN: 978-1-961416-09-3 (sc)
ISBN: 978-1-961416-10-9 (ebk)

I

t's the year 2041. Samantha is at the salon—but why is she at the salon?—she called her boyfriend. Her boyfriend, Cory, was already on one of those snazzy flights to Buenos Aires, Argentina, from Mexico City, Mexico, after the first colony to Mars was established. She went down the hallway through her place and wandered out the doorway with a bottle of tequila in hand.

The ticket to the flight to Buenos Aires, Argentina, was handed to her at the taxi, and she was escorted by two men at the compliments of her former boss. She wisped into and passed the electronic doors opening and closing. And she came into the grandiosity of the terminal with colored stained-glass windows and the murals of the first flight to Mars.

A man at solitary counter quasi-beckoned at her through the dancing and bouncing of the afternoon sun. She started to walk to him and did not hesitate to leave the ticket around her neck in the sleeve of one of the electronic cards. She fingered it. She started to sweat. It was not her first flight, but something close to it. She was flying from Mexico City to Buenos Aires. The man gazed down at his console.

Before she arrived at the console, she made the decision whether or not to address the man. She silently swiped the electronic ticket card holder in front of him. The man continued to look down at the information before him. An around-the-world trip was just confirmed from Mexico City.

She asked, "Do you think a woman flies these days?"

The man continued to look down at this console. And, he said, "No, I do not."

She glared at him. She eased past the console and knew her baggage was already waiting on the plane. She wanted to say something to him, but she did not know what she wanted to say to him.

She walked through the jet tube to the plane. She boarded it. She looked around and she was all alone on the plane from Mexico City to Buenos Aires, Argentina. She did not think that something was wrong maybe nobody else simply had a ticket. She eased into a passenger seat in the front of the plane and put on her beauty mask. The pilot sounded the traditional "all passengers boarded and prepare for takeoff to your destination" speech.

Samantha fell asleep for a while, and she brought out the new device call an abstynth. She turned it on and found her location way up in the sky as she approached Buenos Aires, Argentina. The plane began to land, and when it started to taxi, she disobediently got up from her passenger seat and headed to the door.

"Excuse me, madame, but you need to return to your seat as the plane continues to taxi to the terminal," said the attendant.

Samantha did not politely roll her eyes but waved her hand over the abstynth. It said the plane would be at the terminal in five minutes. She looked out a nearby window at the clear blue skies of Buenos Aires, Argentina.

"Patience is a virtue, deary," she said to the flight attendant.

"Well," said the flight attendant, "you obviously are a woman of success and rapport is too much for you."

Samantha felt weary about another exchange like this one in Mexico City. She was only here to fulfill her bosses' wishes and the wishes of her boyfriend, Cory. The plane finally taxied to the terminal, and the air pressure of the plane gave way to an open door. She began to walk through the jet portal to the terminal and her long legs glanced through her jacket. When she emerged from the jet portal, she found Cory sitting politely at a table.

nd God became true to Cory and Samantha. His Levi's shirt was on the floor. Samantha quickly answered her phone. It was Paris.

Paris was in the adjacent room in the Buenos Aires Hotel. Samantha overheard Paris's boss calling her name. She looked over at Cory and apologized in spirit. Paris was caught by his boss trying to manage the final people on a flight to Rio de Janeiro, Brazil, to Buenos Aires, Argentina. Buenos Aires buzzed with traffic. After the flight, Paris made his way to the corporate office of Styex. He was greeted by a receptionist.

"Welcome," she said.

"Just another day for me, Melissa," said Paris. "Do you have my file and data sharer?" said Paris.

Melissa replied, "Yes, I do." He sneered.

He passed by a television of a military conflict off the coast of Africa near Senegal. A colleague patted Paris on the back. He handed him a paper.

"Congratulations, Paris," he said. "Another successful mission in Africa."

Paris was the CEO of Styex. Paris Pharrell inherited the massive corporation from his father, Scott Pharrell. He was busy protecting it from a potential strike as a monopoly from politicians in Argentina. He tried calling his friends Cory and Samantha. Such a ménage à trois between all them. All three knew that they were cheating between the three of them. But for some reason, it was the appeal of vulnerability and impending doom. For some reason, Paris could not shake the two from him. He had dinner plans with them. The company was doing fine, but the dark clouds on the horizon were serious.

He called them.

"Hey, Cory, what about duck on Paisano Street at 7:00 p.m. with Samantha," exclaimed Paris.

Cory was busy with the holographic abstynth. He was playing one of those addictive games. Cory and Samantha were in a hotel room across the street from the massive headquarters of Styex. They dressed together. They did everything together. Samantha looked at her abstynth. A publicist was contacting her. She accessed the message with her retina. The message did not disagree with her gray matter or any matter in her brain. It only stated that it was likely to go public about her relationship with Cory and the ménage à trois with Paris.

In the room of the hotel was one of those screens that replaced the television about a decade ago. War had broken out in Madagascar, a place critical for the study of anthropology for inhabitation of space and, above all, the corporate profits of Styex. Samantha managed to slip on a dress, and Cory straightened on a tie. They were ready for an epic meeting with Paris Pharrell—their friend and, until recently, accompaniment to the most pleasurable experiences in life.

Paris was sitting at a table with napkins and candles in the middle of the restaurant. The rest of the place was empty. He wanted it intimate. Cory and Samantha waltzed into the restaurant. Samantha had a small purse and necklace of pearls from some bygone era. Cory was wearing an emerald brooch on his tie. They made their way to the table. Paris smiled.

"I'm glad to see both of you. Come sit down," he said.

"Paris Pharrell, you know you have always meant well despite all these conflagrations throughout the globe," said Samantha.

"Quit cutting to the chase, Samantha," said Cory.

"Hmmm…the chase…Who's chasing…and well other dilemmas I refuse to mention," said Paris.

"What do you mean?" said Samantha.

"Well, let's enjoy the duck and put aside more serious matters," said Paris.

Well, the serious matter came. Shortly after they had landed in Buenos Aires, war was declared on the different sectors of the world. The nation state system had failed a long time ago. The dinner lasted for over an hour. All three rose from the table. Samantha fainted, but Paris caught her. When she came to, she dabbed her face with a napkin, and her lip quivered in hope that she was not spotted crying. Soon the media would be ever in front of the restaurant. Cory was shaken by the news Paris told him and Samantha. Paris Pharrell, the leader of Styex and the future of space exploration, was being sent off to war. Neither Samantha nor Cory knew what to make of it. Samantha was in an opal green dress, and Cory in a traditional suit. Paris was as usual unorthodox. He was clothed in one of them—one of those futuristic suits. He always was exclaiming his father's wish and his that we pursue space exploration. All three made their way to the restaurant door. And, then, came the barrage of photographers, flashes of light, and questions from notorious journalists.

"Do you have any idea who the enemy is now?" one journalist exclaimed.

Another shouted, "Paris Pharrell, the economic markets are in roils, and we are lacking the newest monetary exchange called absolute credit for the poor and middle classes. What do you have to say?"

"All I have to say…I hope we aren't experiencing the Western world in 1918," said Paris Pharrell.

Samantha dabbed her eyes. She just wanted this to be over, including these interviews. She knew someone was up to something with the three of them, but she could not put her finger on it. She was gradually told everything. Styex stock and some of the economic markets and experiments supporting the push to space were either collapsing or in disarray.

Cory guided Samantha as they walked down the stairs and away from the journalists and photographers. Cory whispered something into Samantha's ear. There was a limousine to take them to another well-guarded and opulent hotel. All three of them got into the limousine.

As soon as they got into a room on the eighteenth floor of the hotel, Cory said, "Who do you think it was, Paris? It was someone to send you off to war."

"Was it someone in Styex?" said Samantha.

Paris did not want to get into this with Samantha and Cory. He could only think of a couple of people. Styex had an old nemesis called Rubion Corporation, but the CEO had recently died and only left his son, Nicholas Stonis. Nick was not the type to be swayed by the Argentinian politicians and trick him into war. He was currently married to a former employee of Paris, Jennifer Certz.

To put it bluntly, Paris was stunned and it showed; his face was ghostly white. He looked to the screen. More conflagrations were announced as news that Paris Pharrell was sent to war and the markets were in roils. There were no legitimate governments on Earth, and what most people were functioning and harking on was hope.

aris woke up in bed alone in one of his apartments. He had an abstynth on hand; a message was on it. He was to report to the nearest base. He tossed in bed for a bit. Yesterday was overwhelming for him. He sat up in bed and looked around. His fish tank full of cichlids were still going strong, and he wondered who would take care of them when he was gone. Paris turned on the screen. Newer armored and flying vehicles were being shown to the world. Paris threw his legs out of bed and then stood up next to it. He started to stretch. He wondered who he was going to meet today. He tried to contact his secretary and someone left a message. It was Samantha. She sounded a bit despondent. Paris decided to take a shower.

A couple of minutes later, someone called him. A small screen was patched on in the shower for Paris. It was a general. His name was Sturgey.

"Welcome to Unit 231, Paris," he said in a comforting tone. "By the end of the day, you're going to be combat ready," said Sturgey. "Your résumé is astounding. Well, that is expected, given you were the CEO of Styex," he said.

"What are the areas of combat?" Paris said.

"Well, not the same historical front as Europe and Asia," said Sturgey. "You've been assigned the outer rim of Brazil and outside of Africa by Senegal," said Sturgey.

"How many have been called to duty?" said Paris.

"About half a million have been called to serve," said Sturgey.

Paris got out of the shower and put on some modest clothes. He wondered if he could go early to the barracks.

"Can I go early to the barracks?" said Paris. "Sure," said Sturgey.

Paris was ready and shut off the screen. He knew he was being rude to the general, but he was still the CEO of Styex. He grabbed a glass of water and threw it back and drank it. He grabbed a jacket because it was slightly cold outside. He went down the stairs to his brand-new car. It was an electric car with backup solar panels in case the batteries died.

He went into the car, and he zoomed up to the barracks on the other side of Buenos Aires. By ten o'clock at night, he was standing before Sturgey. He was ready to be debriefed. A lot of Styex corporate people and some of his own personal stock were behind Paris's involvement in the war. Paris new what Sturgey wanted him. Sturgey was going to turn him into one of those Mec Warriors. Those soldiers who were changed from an actual human being to a biological and mechanical force to penetrate the lines of whoever is plunging the globe into war.

Paris was prepared to suit up. He passed by Sturgey and looked at one of the suits that stood up against a wall.

Sturgey chimed in to the epic moment. "Perhaps you're forgetting something, Paris," he said. "You need to be linked up, so give me your hand."

Paris did so. And in one fell swoop of technological wonder, Paris was branded with something that looked equivalent to a tattoo that had the ability to link up to the suit at the slightest touch of Paris.

Paris jumped up and down a bit; excited that he was selected to put on the suit. He jumped in. The suit was amazing. His hand linked up and adhered to the tendrils of the suit, and the cerebral interface accessed his memories, emotions, and kinesiological functioning. It was attuned to every soldier. It also had the ability of suborbital space flights and prototypes were in existence that had the ability to take the soldier to Mars. The suits hood closed in around Paris's face.

Paris felt a slight jolt when the suit further linked up to his brain. He felt a longing that may not be replaced. The suit was moving fast. It was already doing a retinal scan. It was that feeling of nostalgia…of almost lost. Did the suit find he was in love and he did not know it? Who was it now? Paris, with the help of the suit, came to the conclusion that he was still in love with Samantha. What was he to do? By the morning, he was off to battle on the front lines on the outer rim of Brazil.

he battlefield known as the Outer Rim of Brazil encompassed all of Rio de Janeiro and the surrounding waterfront. Paris's suit calibrated to the surrounding temperature. He was on the beach. The enemy was cited. They were also Mec Warriors. The enemy had somehow managed to steal Styex's technology to start this war. Paris geared up and armed his weapon. He shot an ion beam and exploded a couple of enemy Mec Warriors. The battlefield was strewn with debris of dead Mec Warriors and simple soldiers.

He wondered what was the agenda of all this fighting. What was the enemy's purpose with Styex? He must find the answer. Paris had only heard rumors that enemies wanted to start a global conflict and halt humanity's advance to space. But why? Styex and a couple of other corporations were close to humanity's final push to Mars and the stars. Paris started to look through the debris. He must find a signal device that will tell him more information about the enemy's advances. He wondered about Samantha and Cory.

He linked up a signal device and plugged into his suit. A map of the world popped up, and it glowed and showed the advances throughout the world in China, India, Saudi Arabia, and Africa. Paris must put a stop to them. He knew they were after Styex's technologies. He glanced over and down at Mec Warriors a couple hundred feet from him. He stared and was startled that one of the Mec Warriors was from the Rubion Corporation.

How could this be? Paris thought. He knew Nicholas Stonis and him were on extremely bad terms because of the war, but he did not think they were bad enough for him to join the enemy to stop humanity's advances to the stars.

Paris tore the Rubion Corporation Mec Warrior's signal device and somehow managed to link it up to his suit. It told him everything. Nicholas Stonis and Jennifer Certz were mentioned in the message from this Mec Warrior. The intelligence sounded like the enemy was growing frightened and was only attacking from lack of resources and also political instability. But why? Paris continued to trudge through the beach and debris of this current battle.

There was much in Paris's way of calling it quits and heading back behind the lines to possibly Montevideo, Uruguay. He must find Samantha and Cory. They must have done some research and found out more about the political breakdown and war. Sweating, Paris gazed around the beach. The sun glimmered and bounced of the waves of Rio de Janeiro. Too bad the beaches of Rio de Janeiro were now littered with bodies of Mec Warriors and soldiers. Paris fired up his jet propulsion system, but it quickly stopped working. Instead, Paris armed a beacon and an evacuation ship came to him to take him to Montevideo, Uruguay.

It took about two hours to reach Montevideo but with little or no enemy fire caught by Paris on his way. He landed on another beach besides the great skyline of Montevideo. He must find Samantha and Cory, he continually repeated to himself. Paris touched his hand and sent out a signal to call on Samantha and Cory. They responded. They were in one of Styex's old buildings on the beachfront of Montevideo. Paris breathed with relief.

VI

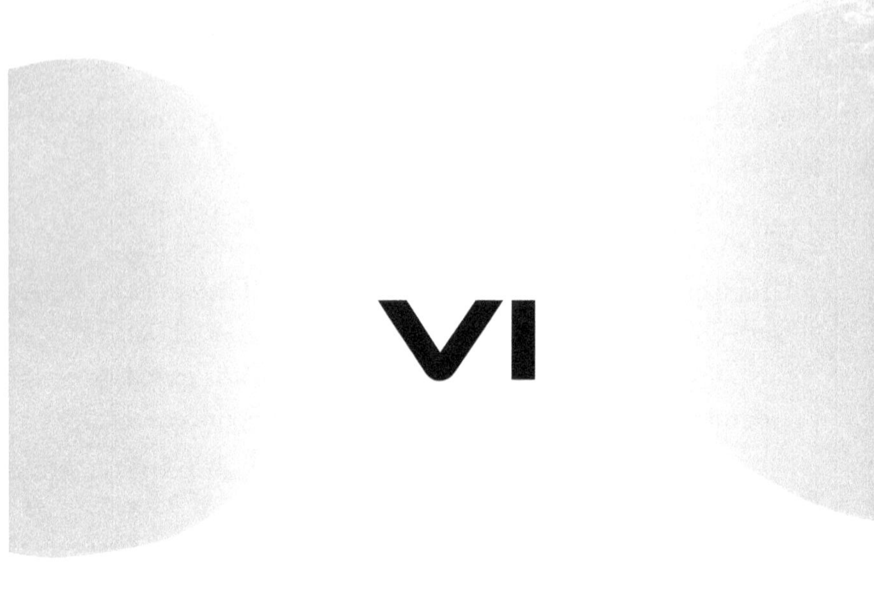

aris disembarked from his suit. He left it against a wall of an old building with some graffiti on it. The suit powered down. He was excited to meet Samantha and Cory. Sand fell through his toes as he walked down the beach and onto a porch where Samantha and Cory were. Samantha's face glowed and her blond hair glistened in the light of the Southern Hemisphere. Cory smiled. It seemed like they had accomplished their mission.

A tablet was on the table between them. Samantha let out a laugh. She always was so lighthearted. Born in a dystopia, all three of them, but this time the twilight of what was left of the utopia was hanging in the balance. Cory was one of them. Paris knew this. Cory was a hope-filled friend—a scientist, a fighter, and all you can be in a man. Paris went through a retinal scan from the table for symptoms of PTSD. None were found.

"What did you find out, Cory and Samantha?" said Paris. "Well, everything," cooed Samantha.

"Yes, Paris," said Cory, "We found out who the treacherous group of people were who plunged the Earth into global warfare. The catalyst was Rubion Corporation led by Nicholas Stonis and his partner, Jennifer Certz.

"You may have remembered them from a couple of soirees before tensions got too high in Buenos Aires and throughout the globe," continued Cory. Paris nodded. He remembered both of them. Nicholas was an old friend, and Jennifer was a past sexual conquest. But Paris had yet to learn his lesson with these three. Paris's dad, Scott Pharrell, may have been right. Paris was too awash with money and did not have the moral capability to have enough foresight to see the coming doom.

"Now that I did some of my first duties," said Paris, "what have we found out you two?"

"The typical," said Cory. "Rubion Corporation and their leaders, Nicholas and Jennifer, are playing to continually plunge the world into global warfare and stop our push to Mars."

"Is there a catch?" said Paris.

"The catch is the moon. It's still a stopping point to push to Mars. We will stop them there," said Cory.

"Well, I understand, how in imminent danger humanity is, but what I don't understand, Paris and Cory, is how they breached and plunged us into this global war," chided Samantha.

Paris reluctantly winked. "Well, it's clear they sabotaged the markets and all the major corporations and found out that while we were prospering, half the world was sleeping on the eve of prosperity and the greatest victory of their time," said Paris.

"What is next?" said Samantha. "There must be more to this, and we have to stop it."

Cory held a deck of cards in his hands and tossed a card to Samantha. "Are you forgetting he said that life is a gamble?" he said.

"Our only hope is to infiltrate Rubion Corporation and put a stop to the war," said Cory.

"I understand, Cory," said Samantha. "Dashing good looks on all three of us. They are not going to save him from the fate of getting more than slightly bit dirty."

Paris laughed. "I vote for Cory to stay here to hold down the base of Styex Corporation. We still have some employees here despite the evacuations from Buenos Aires. You're smart, Cory, and if you have to serve in a firefight, the enemy will be in for it and about the power behind Styex Corporation," said Paris.

"Now that we have our individual missions figured out on Earth," said Cory. "What about what is going up in space?"

"I feel that will be left up to me," said Paris. "My suit is already Martian ready, and I can be transported there with me in it."

"What will you find when you get there?" said Samantha.

"I'll find the marvelous. And by that I meant what is left of Styex and the other corporations who built Mars before total warfare broke out amongst the corporations and on Earth."

"I get it," said Samantha. "I'm going to be assigned to the moon. The crucial base jump to Mars."

"Yes," said Paris.

"The moon is yours, Samantha," said Paris. "And what lies there, I hope, will be friendly."

"Well, I don't think that is much different than you going alone to Mars just in a suit without accompaniment," she said.

The sun started to go down on them in Montevideo, Uruguay. They had spent the better part of the late afternoon discussing their futures before they fully encounter the war. Cory took down some final notes. Even though there were three of them, the success of Paris's mission was crucial. The three had spent most of their lives together, and now they are being separated to fight for their lives. Cory sent a last dispatch to Styex headquarters to see if they had received any word of Rubion Corporation, Nicholas Stonis, or Jennifer Certz and there was none.

VII

Despite the lack of communication about Rubion Corporation, Samantha walked to Styex headquarters alone. Her mission given by the other two was to arrive at the moon and access the computers of Rubion Corporation. It was a hope of Samantha's that the moon not be guarded.

Samantha was on the thirtieth floor of the Styex Corporation. She sat down by a computer and listened attentively to a recording of Nicholas Stonis and Jennifer Certz, the leaders of Rubion Corporation. It sounded like they had left at the beginning of the war. Samantha further accessed a computer and decided which type of ship to board to the moon. She touched her stomach. She groaned. She feared that she had contracted a virus on the beaches of Montevideo.

She went into an adjacent room and got undressed to get rid of the dirty clothes from earlier in the day. She put on a Styex uniform. It fit. She was ready for launch. Samantha found a ship, and the accelerator turned on to power the flight to the moon. She looked at the console and pushed the commencement button. In about fifteen minutes, she arrived at the moon. She docked with what look like a Rubion docking area. After the docking was secure, she started the job. She must hurry; by this time, Paris was already preparing for launch Mars.

Samantha turned on an abstynth and encoded where she was, and it decoded where the main headquarters of the Rubion Corporation was. It was directly ahead. She asked the abstynth if there were any life signs and none were reported. Suddenly, Samantha stopped. The pain in her stomach was getting worse, but she must complete the mission. She walked into the headquarters of Rubion Corporation. It was massive. And there was a screen of Earth with enemy military movements on it. They were clearly in on the collapse of Earth. But Styex and Paris Pharrell must know why.

Suddenly, a pain entered the left arm of Samantha. She was surprised. A cackle was heard across the room on the second level of the balcony. "And you thought you could stop Nicholas and me, the rest of the corporations, and enemies from making the final push to space impossible," said Jennifer Certz.

"Yes, it's not about *if* we thought we could stop you. It's about when and why did you do it. Why did you plunge the Earth into global war?" said Samantha.

"Perhaps you do not know heartache yet," said Jennifer. "If I give you the code to the Rubion headquarters, would you leave?" she said. "The deed has been done to you," said Certz.

"What do you mean?" said Samantha.

"Hmmm…Perhaps…you're mistaken what true heartache has been in these tumultuous times, Samantha," said a voice in a chair across the room.

The chair turned and there was Nicholas Stonis, the leader of Rubion Corporation. He was just in normal Earth attire. I guess he found no need to be flashy.

Samantha shouted, "We just wanted to know why you plunged the Earth into a global war!"

"We plunged the Earth into a global war because it was sleeping. You, Samantha, and your group knew that you were living on Earth, but instead chose to sleep. What or who would you give birth to now?" sneered Nicholas. "We will soon find out," he said.

Nicholas walked closer to Samantha. "Just give me your finger, and we will be done with this exchange of inimical words, Samantha," said Nicholas. Samantha gave him her finger.

"Ah, look what…I mean…whom do we have here?" said Nicholas. "What do you mean?" said Samantha.

"Ah, you're giving birth to a baby boy," said Nicholas.

"I thought you were willing to trade information or something about your plot to plunge the world further into war," said Samantha.

"Plunge?" said Nicholas. "Too much collateral damage would be taken to continue this war. I had a better idea. It would be better to rule Earth, Mars, and space…well…through you Samantha…through your child," he said. "You what?" said Samantha.

"Take her away, guards," said Nicholas. "The future ruler has been pronounced. And well, you'll just give birth, Samantha, in an accelerated process," said Nicholas.

VIII

aris landed on Mars in his militaristic suit. On Mars, some of the cities were in ruins. The city Paris was situated in was Steg 2, and it was running amok with refugees. As soon as Paris saw a refugee cower to him and hid, he locked and loaded his weapon and blew through a couple of enemies with his ion beam. "Run to the nearest evacuation effort," he told the refugee. Paris was trying to assess the damage done by the ground troops and the aerial bombardment from space. The damage was significant. He was here to try to find the rest of the corporations and a few Rubion leaders to put an end to the war on Earth.

He needed to find their base. On the horizon, Steg 2 was basically up in flames. He maneuvered away from the heat of the flames even though he was more than a couple of miles from the heat. He continued to move to what seemed like a base. It appeared to be located on what a pristine part of the city completes with fountains, murals, and skyscrapers with futuristic architecture that people from Earth would look on with envy.

It took a while, but within a couple of hours, he was inside the Rubion base. He made his way to the twelfth floor of the base. He looked around the room he was in. Currently, there were the Rubion corporations, its leaders, and all other enemies tracking the inhabitants of Mars as refugees from this room in the base. Paris just shook his head. He knew it was now time to stop them. He looked over the complicated console controlling Steg 2 and outlying regions. He pressed a code on the suit of his arm and then linked it up to the console and the tracking device on the refugees was shut down.

Paris heard a whimpering noise. He looked around and was jostled. He looked down. It was a refugee child. The boy was crying. He thought of Samantha. The boy had tired eyes and looked as if he had been scavenging around for food.

"Do you have family?" said Paris.

"No," he sobbed. "They were murdered in a firefight."

The outright evil of Rubion's plot to put a stop to humanity's push to Mars and the stars Paris now felt. As the CEO and a leader from Earth, Paris felt he was on the right, but he wished Earth had been more organized. Maybe Rubion was right. The despair of humanity's attempt to inhabit the stars had been felt. Rubion was one of the economic pessimists behind all this effort to inhabit space and colonize Mars and Styex was by far an optimistic. Paris looked at a patch on the arm of the child. It has a patch from Styex. Paris cried and punched the console with the metallic hand given to him by the suit.

He knew that one of the three of them mattered. Was it Cory or Samantha? He knew it must be Samantha. Paris did feel guilty about how they handled the disintegration of Earth, but the corporations and especially Styex could hold on no more. They were already becoming and practicing despotic and nepotic policies. If they had not, there would be nothing left of Earth. Earth's resources were almost exhausted. Samantha was one of those few utopian voices.

He never understood why she was one of the them: a utopian. She was a visionary. She saw hope when there was not. The child stopped sobbing, and as soon as he did, another child appeared from behind a door across the room. He decided to take the two to the nearest evacuation effort. The newest child had the same Styex patch on his arm.

After battling through Steg 2, Paris remembered odd memories come about before the end. Was Samantha the one to spend the rest of his life with? He understood the tension between the three of them as board members of Styex, but the sudden attack and economic decline showed everything to them and proved the frailty of the corporate way and the past economic system.

IX

ory was still at base in Buenos Aires, Argentina. There was scant word from Samantha but plenty of communication was coming in from Paris. Cory was not waiting on anything in particular from either Samantha or Paris. All he was told to do was basically hold down the fort in case the enemy decided to overrun Buenos Aires.

There were reports outside Buenos Aires and close to Montevideo that the enemy made an advance. But Cory thought nothing of it. Cory knew that Samantha and Paris had to move fast or else. Cory could not keep his thoughts together recently. He was struggling to admit to the current situation. He missed the old way of life. He missed the calm, the partying, and the opulent way of life.

Cory stumbled across some old manuscripts from a university professor who fled at the beginning of the fighting. The professor started a paper with "*What was our world?*" And another one "*Was our world sleeping?*" The professor clearly felt the advances in technologies, and breaking the frontier to Mars and space was not leading our civilization to catastrophe, but something was. What was it sleeping on?

Cory was still a good friend of Paris, so he decided to forward some of these manuscripts and send them across space to Paris on Steg 2. Maybe there was an answer there. Was it up to us—the human beings—who had fallen asleep in our opulent way of life? Clearly the enemy found a strategic vulnerability.

Cory just received word from Paris. He looked on the screen of a computer. Paris was bringing a couple of refugee children and maybe more along for the ride to Earth. Were the children the key? Cory did not want to sound creepy to himself, but there had to be a reason why our world was failing. Maybe one of the children was the answer.

Cory had not thought about the Rubion Corporation but thought what made them so mighty. Of course, they plunged the world into global warfare, and to the best of Cory's assessment, it keeps plunging. Cory decided to access Samantha and Cory's files sent by Styex's headquarters. There must be a reason as to why Rubion Corporation and its enemies attacked.

Nicholas Stonis and Jennifer Certz complained that the world of Cory, Samantha, and Paris was sleeping. Was it some kind of vendetta that they unleased this global catastrophe?

Cory's mind drifted. At the beginning, Cory did not mind being stuck in the fray of ménage à trois. It fitted the opulent times. He often took a step back when they were conversing.

Cory received communication from Samantha. It was scant. And it sounded like there was scuffling and words being exchanged. Cory knew that Samantha was on the moon, trying to figure out who the real enemy was. If it was Jennifer Certz and Nicholas Stonis, the two of them were in for it. There must have been a reason they did what they did to plunge the Earth into global warfare.

Cory received a communiqué from Samantha. And it read, "I'm pregnant."

But by who? he thought. Samantha and the three of them had not had sexual intercourse as of late. Did Nicholas and Jennifer find out and use the pregnancy against Samantha? What was the point to that? There must be a secret.

Cory automatically sent some troop assistance to Samantha to protect her and the baby. Jennifer and Nicholas were up to something. And Cory knew whatever was about to happened, whatever revelation that was about to happen, was going to be a gigantic one.

X

amantha was taken to a not-well-furnished room inside the Rubion Corporation located on the moon. Nicholas threw her on a table, and Samantha vomited in return. Jennifer Certz appeared on the other side of the table.

"Are you ready for an accelerated birth process?" said Jennifer. "What?" said Samantha. "I thought it was natural."

"Not this time or ever," said Jennifer.

Samantha started to groan with the pains of birth, and her eyes rolled back inside her head. Jennifer and Nicholas left the room with a nurse and doctor. After birth, the baby was taken from Samantha. She wanted to know why she gave birth and why Nicholas, Jennifer, and the Rubion Corporation did this to Earth and the future of humanity. Samantha just realized she was under the influence of a retinal scan.

"Well, you may get your wish now that I have your baby to learn the reason why we did what we did. Well, I mean my baby and Nicholas's and all the gene splicing two mighty corporations—well one is former—can provide," said Jennifer.

"What do you mean?" screamed Samantha. "We are innocent."

"Au contraire," exclaimed Jennifer. "Far from innocence came out of your womb."

"What?" continued to scream Samantha. "It's a living human being."

Samantha grabbed a hold on something pinning her down. She ripped it apart and grabbed the other one with her hand. She set herself free.

"Now tell me, Jennifer, what did you do with the baby?" she said. "Nicholas! She's escaping!" yelled Jennifer.

Jennifer tapped a stolen abstynth. Nicholas sent a message to meet him in lobby overseeing a lab. The baby was in the lab.

Samantha made her way to the lab. Nicholas and Jennifer were there, mesmerized by the military advances all over Earth, in space, and Mars. Nicholas and Jennifer were beside a medical pod with the baby in it.

Samantha stood silently before them.

"And you wondered why we did what we have been doing and what we did to you, Samantha," said Nicholas. "It's simple."

"You poisoned our lands on Mars and on Earth. You made our children mine the hollow crust of the moon. Styex Corporation and its model of a man of Paris took everything for granted. What kind of leadership was that? We, the rest of humanity, demanded new leadership and I provided it," said Nicholas.

"You're mad," said Samantha. "There was no reason to impregnate me or try to give point when there is none between you and me after what you've done. Is that the reason you plunged the Earth into global war?" said Samantha.

"Perhaps you did not understand how boundless love is," said Nicholas. "When I found out Jennifer was almost poisoned, I spent months trying to

find a way to have a child. And no hosts sufficed. There was just one, and it was you. Samantha," he said.

"I know what Cory is going to say," said Jennifer. "He is going to take your side."

"He knows what we are up to," said Nicholas.

As soon as they said that, Cory burst through the door with group of soldiers fully fitted even to take on a Mec Warrior. Cory surveyed the area. He started to cry.

"Samantha, over here," said Cory. "I know what your filth are doing," said Cory. "You're planning to infiltrate Styex Corporation with a child from the womb of Samantha. You plan to rule over Earth with him and, after you're gone, have him rule Earth and Mars and his descendants."

"Well, Cory, perhaps you're not mistaken," said Nicholas.

"There is no remedy to this situation," said Jennifer. "You might as well give up."

"We'll see who wins. Paris has yet to live up to his name," said Nicholas.

Paris managed to get a beacon, which signaled that Cory and Samantha were on the moon with a hidden base of the Rubion Corporation uncovered. Paris had no idea what was going on or what he was getting himself into at the moment. Cory sent a signal on his abstynth to Paris.

Paris acknowledged it. Both Cory and Samantha were safe. Paris walked through the lobby where a lab was located. Nicholas Stonis was sitting in a chair and Jennifer Certz was standing alongside him.

"Ah, Paris Pharrell, looks like you were prepared to sacrifice your life to save others. Anyone in particular? Despite the refugee scum," said Nicholas.

"No," said Paris, and he still felt like punching him.

Paris heard a cry. He could not tell where it was coming from. In the lab? Was it Samantha?

"Do you value all life, Paris?" said Nicholas. "Well, during these beyond difficult times, including yourself," said Nicholas.

"Yes, I do," said Paris.

"Ugh. You are not the same as when you came from Mars," said Nicholas. "Perhaps…Was it the Mars cannon fodder clinging onto your suit?" said Nicholas.

"Just stay away from them," said Paris. He ushered the refugee children to the door away from a potential fight. He looked over at Samantha. She was cuddling something. He could barely tell what it was. Until he finally discerned correctly it was a baby. But from who, from Cory or someone else?

"Ah, I see you noticed the infant," said Nicholas. "And may I be more precise, *your* infant, Paris Pharrell. Just take it as a gift from the enemy. One which lies the future too *everything*," said Nicholas.

"What do you mean *everything*?" said Paris. "A baby is just a baby. You're saying choice has already started with him, but I don't understand."

"Ah, you almost sound too antiquated," said Nicholas. "In a couple years of accelerated growth processes, the baby, John Pharrell, will be the size of his father, Paris Pharrell," said Nicholas.

"And as for his uncle, Nicholas Stonis, from a divorced marriage without the opulent heirlooms and contracts to Styex, I concur that you deserve the child, brother," said Nicholas.

Paris still felt like punching his brother, Nicholas, or sending an ion beam through him.

"Paris!" said Samantha. "Control your anger! John Pharrell, the baby, will be fine."

"What about the future of the child?" said Paris. "I doubt extremely you did this in my best interest. Did you want money? What did you want? You know Mother and Father left you out of the will, the corporation, the potential of the right to rule Earth and Mars," said Paris.

"I know things got complicated, but there was no need to do this. You put Samantha's life at risk and Cory's. There is a far greater enemy approaching us," said Paris.

"Oh, really, enlighten me," said Nicholas.

"Enlighten you? Earth, Mars, and humanity's attempts into space are almost in ruins. What do you have to say for yourself, Nicholas and Jennifer?" said Paris.

"What are you going to do with the two of us, brother? There are the courts. Oh, how great, there are the courts. A failure automatically. They are," said Nicholas.

"I do not believe the courts will decide. The baby, soon to be child, will be raised with me," said Paris.

"Ah, to keep him from his uncle," said Nicholas. "From his maddened uncle that is," said Paris.

"Paris, we must leave now. Buenos Aires and Earth are rioting. They need food," said Samantha. "Cory, take the baby on the nearest ship from the moon to Buenos Aires," said Samantha. "I'll deal with Nicholas and Jennifer," said Paris

Cory, the baby, and other children went down some stairs.

"Do you know why, brother, the world was half-sleeping when Rubion Corporation took control of Earth, Mars, and dare I say, the moon as well?" said Nicholas.

"Yes, I never gave it a thought," said Paris. "I thought the world was just being the world."

"Ah, brother, you never knew at your apogee, at your decadence, there was a watcher which spotted us, brother," said Nicholas.

"What do you mean?" said Paris.

"There has been a watcher, Paris, on our doings on Earth, Mars, and the moon. And like, any older harsh-minded brother, I went for the harsh-minded business. That was the only way to tell you we were about to be invaded not from each other, but from another far more treacherous enemy."

"I don't believe you," said Paris.

"I thought he wouldn't," chimed in Jennifer.

"Then, what is the actual plot? Then why did you bring in Samantha and I into this to conceive a child?" said Paris.

"Well, it was only fitting. Our mother and father left us everything, and it spoiled us a bit. Until things very recently came apart at the seams," said Nicholas.

"The Watchers, as Jennifer and I call them, are not interested in us at all. They are only interested in conquering us. Senseless really. They seem to be as senseless as my vendetta to use you and lure you to tell you this in my despair."

"But why despair, Nicholas? We could have done it together." Paris sounded increasingly despondent.

"Well, I didn't want to give the Watchers their trophy. My brother would be their trophy to be exact," said Nicholas. "But…oh stop…you're the…little brother," said Nicholas. "The deal has been done between you and I. And if you die in the coming war, firefight, or whatever, you will have an heir, and Mother and Father's dynasty will be intact."

"But what about your dream of the Rubion Corporation?" said Paris.

"That was nothing but a ruse. For one, it kept your older brother from going crazy. And once I spotted the Watchers, I decided to flip the markets and do everything plausible to teach your beyond spoiled self that the enemy is here," said Nicholas.